Sally Noll

THAT BOTHERED KATE

PUFFIN BOOKS

PUFFIN BOOKS
Published by the Penguin Group
Penguin Books USA Inc., 375 Hudson Street, New York, New York 10014, U.S.A.
Penguin Books Ltd, 27 Wrights Lane, London W8 5TZ, England
Penguin Books Australia Ltd, Ringwood, Victoria, Australia
Penguin Books Canada Ltd, 10 Alcorn Avenue, Toronto, Ontario, Canada M4V 3B2
Penguin Books (N.Z.) Ltd, 182–190 Wairau Road, Auckland 10, New Zealand

Penguin Books Ltd, Registered Offices: Harmondsworth, Middlesex, England

First published in the United States of America by Greenwillow Books,
a division of William Morrow & Company, Inc., 1991
Published in Puffin Books, 1993

3 5 7 9 10 8 6 4 2

LIBRARY OF CONGRESS CATALOGING-IN-PUBLICATION DATA

Noll, Sally.
That bothered Kate / Sally Noll.   p.   cm.
Summary: Kate is bothered by her changing relationship with her little sister
Tory, as first Tory wants to be with her and copy her all the time
and then Tory neglects her for friends of her own.
ISBN 0-14-054885-8
[1. Sisters—Fiction.] I. Title
[PZ7.N725Th   1993]
[E]—dc20   92-40167   CIP   AC

Printed in the United States of America
Set in Neuzeit

For
Kate Alexis
and Victoria Elizabeth,
with love

Kate's little sister, Tory, was a copycat.
And that bothered Kate.

Everything Kate did, Tory wanted to do, too.

Everything.

"It's part of growing up," her mother would assure her. "She needs you."

But there just wasn't anything Kate did
that Tory didn't want to try.

She wanted to look like Kate.

Once their neighbor
Mrs. Potts said,
"My, you look just like twins,"
even though she knew
they weren't.

And that bothered Kate.

Double peppermint chocolate chip
was Kate's favorite ice cream.
It was Tory's favorite, too.

And that bothered Kate the most.

Then one day Alex asked Tory
to ride with him.

The next week Annie from across the street invited Tory to play.

After that Tory and Annie played often...

and sometimes Tory just wanted to play alone.

It seemed to Kate that Tory hardly noticed her.
And that bothered Kate.

"Is this part of growing up, too?"
Kate asked.

"Yes," said her mother. "I am afraid
this is part of growing up, too."

"But she doesn't need me anymore,"
said Kate sadly.
"Oh, yes, she does," said her mother.
"In so many ways. And right now she needs
you to hold her hand crossing the street
while you both go to the
ice cream store."

As they went down the street, Kate asked,
"Tory, what flavor are you going
   to have?"
"Double peppermint chocolate chip,
   of course," said Tory.

And that didn't bother Kate at all.